Understanding Weather

I hope you enjoy learning about the weather!

Best,
Karen Treland Evensen

KAREN TRELAND EVENSEN

Copyright © 2019 Karen Treland Evensen
All rights reserved
First Edition

PAGE PUBLISHING, INC.
New York, NY

First originally published by Page Publishing, Inc. 2019

ISBN 978-1-64214-070-5 (Paperback)
ISBN 978-1-64544-168-7 (Hardcover)
ISBN 978-1-64214-071-2 (Digital)

Printed in the United States of America

Weather—what is it really?

Well, personally, I think it is really cool! (Hee-hee, get it?). Sorry, that was pretty lame.

Actually, weather has to be interesting. It is always changing and never exactly the same. Sometimes it makes you feel good; sometimes it makes you feel blue. Sometimes it's scary, and other times it gets you unglued.

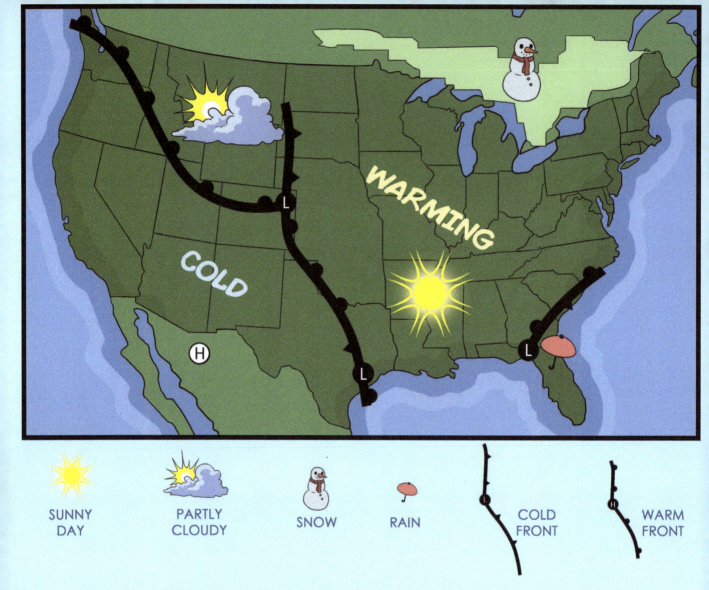

Yesterday we had a weatherman from TV come to my school. He said he was a meteorologist. He showed us all the symbols used on his weather map. Most of the symbols were easy to read, but the lines for cold and warm fronts were new to me. There were also some symbols that looked like a different language!

He said that they usually don't use most of these when they're doing the weather on TV, but, since I showed such an interest, he would explain some of them to me.

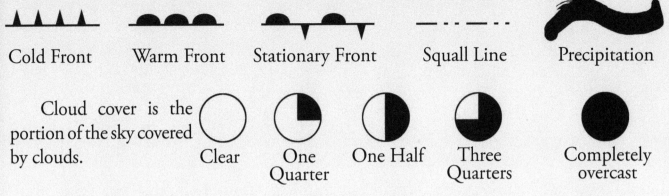

Cold Front Warm Front Stationary Front Squall Line Precipitation

Cloud cover is the portion of the sky covered by clouds.

Clear One Quarter One Half Three Quarters Completely overcast

Wind—the feathers show speed in mph. The end of the arrow with the feathers points in the direction from which the wind is blowing.

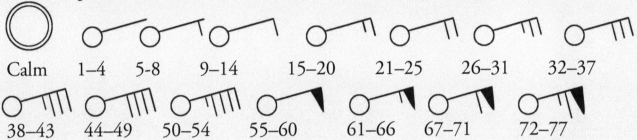

Calm 1–4 5-8 9–14 15–20 21–25 26–31 32–37

38–43 44–49 50–54 55–60 61–66 67–71 72–77

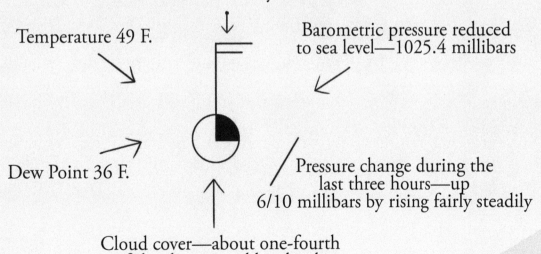

Wind speed and direction
North at fifteen to twenty miles an hour

Temperature 49 F.

Barometric pressure reduced to sea level—1025.4 millibars

Dew Point 36 F.

Pressure change during the last three hours—up 6/10 millibars by rising fairly steadily

Cloud cover—about one-fourth of the sky covered by clouds

    When I wake up in the morning, the first thing I think about is the weather, don't you? All of the different things I see through my window can help me decide what the weather will be today.

    If there are blue skies and it is very bright out, I know it will be a pretty day even if the temperature is cold. Sunshine makes everyone feel good. The sun gives us heat. The longer the sun is shining, the warmer the temperature. When it is really hot out, people say that "you could fry an egg on the sidewalk."

I know you know what rain is, but do you know where it comes from? From the sky, of course. If you look straight up when it is raining, you'll probably get nailed square in the eye with big blops of water!

The clouds up in the sky fill up with drops of water. When the clouds get really full of water, the water droplets (rain) fall from the sky. It goes into the ground, rivers, and oceans. Then the water disappears or "evaporates" back into the air and floats up into the clouds.

The clouds fill up again; then the rain falls again. When it is raining really hard, people call it "raining cats and dogs."

Oh, yeah! If the temperature is thirty-two degrees or lower, the rain gets so cold that it turns into snow, hail, or sleet.

The big word for those things is *precipitation*, which is just moisture that falls to the earth.

Eeeks! One more thing has to do with the sun and the rain. If it is raining and the sun shines through the drops, it makes a rainbow. If you are totally lucky, you may get to see a double rainbow. Wow!

In a rainstorm, instead of seeing a rainbow in the sky, you might see a big bolt of lightning. MAJOR ELECTRICITY! Then comes the thunder … CRAAACKKK BOOM BOOM! Angels bowling? Nice try, Mom. It may sound like that, but what it really is that the hot, hot lightning bolts heat up the air, then that hot air bumps into some cool air, and BLAMMM! Introducing Mr. Thunder, ladies and gentlemen. The noisiest guy in town!

Wind is another part of the weather. Windy days are great for kite flying. A good wind will scoop that son of a gun right up into the sky and KEEP it there. A puny wind might get your kite halfway up, then CRASH! Personally, I go for the good wind days.

Now, when there is major, major wind that twists around in the shape of an ice cream cone (minus the ice cream), it is called a tornado. They can be dangerous and scary. Remember the Wizard of Oz when Auntie Em's house started twirling away up, up in the sky? Tornado, big time. It isn't always that bad, so don't go bonkers every time you hear about a tornado watch on your TV.

Hurricanes are also big-time winds. They start over oceans, getting stronger and twirlier, scooping up the water as they move toward the land. By the time it gets there, it can literally huff and puff and blow your house down!!! While it's huffing and puffing, it is also flooding everything in sight. You can end up with a very, very messy and sad, sopping wet town.

By the way, I probably should tell you what "wind" is. Warm air rises from the earth, then cool air moves in, and the two mix together. The cool air gets warmed, and it also rises. Then more cool air budges in and gets warmed and rises again and again—cool, warm, cool, warm, whoosh, whoosh, WIND!

While you are peeking out your window, check out the clouds. Look at them very carefully. Different shapes mean different kinds of weather.

It's pretty simple. When the sky looks like a big gray blanket, then those clouds are called "stratus." Basically, it means to grab your galoshes cuz rain's a-comin'!

If the sky has "cirrus" clouds, they will be white and feathery. You might want to watch the weather channel because these clouds mean that there could be a change in the weather.

When clouds that look like a huge head of cauliflower (yuck!), I'm glad they stay in the sky. They are big and puffy and called "cumulus." I love looking at these clouds the most. If I stare at one cloud for a long time, I might see a dragon or a man in the moon or a castle. Besides being the funniest clouds, they also mean fair weather … which in secret code is BTBOMB, which translates to BIG-TIME BOOGEYING ON MY BIKE!

Well, speaking of BTBOMB, I just looked out my window and guess what? Cumulus!

Yeah, baby! That means I am also BTOOH—translation, BIG-TIME OUT OF HERE! Bye!

About the Author

Well, let's see. On the original book, the author said Kellie Evensen. Truth be told, this was a high school project for one of our daughters, Kellie, that turned into a fun project for Mom and Dad.

This was a number of years ago, so we don't remember all of the details, but the bottom line was, Mom wrote the book, and Dad did the pictures.

Karen and Gary Evensen have daughters and live in Glen Ellyn, Illinois with their two cats, Zane and Boy Boy. They have two business's in their town named Olive' n Vinnie's and UPTOWN, which are 500 feet from each other. The gourmet food stores offer imported olive oils, balsamics, along with a store full of beautiful other goodies.

Prior to the stores, Gary made his living with his two brothers in a band called The Evans Brothers and Karen worked (and still does, for her mother Joan Treland, a clinical educational specialist). They owned a large Wisconsin supper club called The Cotton Patch with a petting zoo behind the restaurant.

When we told Kellie that we have decided to publish this book because EVERYONE loved it, she was excited and happy that she would be selling this book. The original author was changed from Kellie Evensen to The Evensen Family. She knew better than to argue.

CPSIA information can be obtained
at www.ICGtesting.com
Printed in the USA
BVHW022008221019
561796BV00003B/4/P